# SECRETS OF AN OVERWORLD SURVIVOR

## LOST IN THE JUNGLE

# GREYSON MANN

## ILLUSTRATED BY
## GRACE SANDFORD

Sky Pony Press
New York

Copyright © 2017 by Hollan Publishing, Inc.

Minecraft® is a registered trademark of Notch Development AB.

The Minecraft game is copyright © Mojang AB.

Sky Pony Press books may be purchased in bulk at special discounts for sales
promotion, corporate gifts, fund-raising, or educational purposes. Special
editions can also be created to specifications. For details, contact the Special
Sales Department, Sky Pony Press, 307 West 36th Street, 11th Floor,
New York, NY 10018 or info@skyhorsepublishing.com.

Sky Pony® is a registered trademark of Skyhorse Publishing, Inc.®,
a Delaware corporation.

Minecraft® is a registered trademark of Notch Development AB.
The Minecraft game is copyright © Mojang AB.

Visit our website at www.skyponypress.com.

10 9 8 7 6 5 4 3 2 1

Library of Congress Cataloging-in-Publication Data is available on file.

Special thanks to Erin L. Falligant.

Cover illustration by Grace Sandford
Cover design by Brian Peterson

Hardcover ISBN: 978-1-5107-1325-3
Ebook ISBN: 978-1-5107-1326-0

Printed in the United States of America

Interior design by Joshua Barnaby

# SECRETS OF AN OVERWORLD SURVIVOR

## LOST IN THE JUNGLE

# CHAPTER 1

*This is it,* thought Will. *It's now or never.* He leaned over the fence to scratch the pig's head, and then he reached for the saddle.

*Oops!* He'd almost forgotten the bait. "Wait here," he said to the pig. "I'll be right back."

Will grabbed his fishing pole and hurried to the garden to find a ripe carrot. As he tugged the leafy green end of one from the dirt, the pig grunted.

"Easy, boy," said Will, pressing his fishhook through the carrot. "You can eat it, but not quite yet." Then he hurried back to the pigpen and leaned the fishing pole against the fence. The carrot dangled just out of the pig's reach.

As Will placed his saddle gently on the pig's back, the pig grunted a protest. But he kept his black eyes on that carrot.

Will eased himself over the fence and lowered himself onto the saddle. Then he reached for the fishing pole.

"Okay, boy," he said. "Here we go. Follow the carrot!"

Will held the carrot just in front of the pig's nose, leading him left and right around the pen. The pig moved slowly at first and then began to trot. Will held on tight, laughing out loud. It was working. He was actually riding a pig!

As the animal ran in circles, Will pretended he was a spider jockey. He aimed his bow and arrow—er, fishing pole—at the other pigs in the pen. He released an imaginary arrow. "Gotcha!"

As he whirled around to search for more pigs, he came face to face

with . . . Seth, his older brother. Seth
was running toward the pen, waving
his arms in the air. Was he trying to
say something?

"STOP!" Seth finally cried.
Will dropped the fishing
pole in surprise.

The pig came to a screeching halt in front of the carrot.

And Will sailed over the fence and landed squarely in Seth's pumpkin patch. *Ouch.*

"What are you *doing*?!"  sputtered Seth from the edge of the garden.

"What?" said Seth, squinting. "The jungle? Sure, but lots of monsters creep in the shadows of those tall trees. And it's hard to clear out enough trees to make room to build a house."

Will snorted. *Houses. Of course. That's all Seth can think about.*

As he pushed himself up from the ground, a chunk of pumpkin shell slid off his back. "Well, I want to see it," he said. "The jungle, the desert, the ocean—all of it. And when I'm done, I'll explore the Nether, too."

Seth choked with disbelief. "The Nether? Not many people who visit the Nether live to tell about it, little brother."

"Well, I'll be one of them," said Will, standing tall. "I'll fight the zombie pigmen, the ghasts, the wither skeletons—anything that stands in my way."

Seth made a big brother face—the one that means, *I'll bet you won't.*

So Will added one more thing. "I'm going to see it all," he said. "And I'm leaving *tomorrow*."

# CHAPTER 2

"Can't you wait a few days before leaving?" asked Seth. "Then you'll have time to make a plan." The morning sun peeked over his shoulder from the doorway to Will's hut.

"Nope," said Will. He slung his bag over his shoulder. "I've been dreaming about exploring the Overworld my whole life. If I have to wait another day, I'll explode—like a dirty creeper."

Seth sighed. "Well, at least wait till someone can go with you," he pleaded.

Will shook his head. "I don't need a babysitter. I'm fine on my own."

The boys stared at each other for a moment. Seth was half a head taller, with the same brown skin and dark hair as Will. They looked alike on the outside. But on the inside?

*He's nothing like me,* thought Will. *He'll never understand. But I'm going anyway.* He set his jaw and stood tall.

Seth finally raised his hands in the air. "Okay, have it your way," he said. "But come to my house so I can send a few things with you, like tools and food."

Will almost said no, but then his stomach grumbled. *Food isn't a bad idea,* he thought as he followed Seth toward the black-rock mansion next door.

Seth kept most of his tools in a chest, and he had *a lot* of them.

"You'll want a shovel for digging dirt, an axe for chopping wood, and a pickaxe for mining stone," he said as he pulled out a few tools. He studied the handle of the pickaxe. "Uh-oh. This one's getting worn out."

"That's way too much!" said Will. "I have my sword and my bow and arrow. That's enough."

Seth shook his head. "You can't build a shelter with a sword," he said. "And you're going to need shelter as soon as the sun sets." He stared straight into Will's eyes and added, "Do *not* stay outside at night, when the monsters spawn. It's not safe."

Will knew he was being lectured, but he felt a twinge of excitement. The feeling only grew as he watched Seth pull a pouch of emeralds from the chest. "What are those for?" he asked.

"You can trade them in the village," said Seth, counting out about ten green stones. "Go to the blacksmith shop and ask for an iron pickaxe."

Will held the glittering stones in his palm. He'd never had his own emeralds before! He slid them safely into his pocket.

By the time he set off down the hill, his pack was nearly bursting. He had his wooden sword and his bow and arrow, plus a whole lot more: an axe, a fishing pole, a loaf of golden-brown bread, a few apples, and some fish

A man in a black apron was tending one of the furnaces on the front porch. "Ah," he said, glancing up and wiping the sweat off his brow. "It's the builder's brother!"

Will winced. Here in town, no one knew his name. But they sure knew Seth, the famous builder, who had built the clock tower and several other buildings in Little Oak.

"Um, my name is Will, actually," he said. "I'm here to make a trade. I need an iron pickaxe."

The blacksmith nodded and led the way inside to a large chest. As he lifted the lid, Will saw all sorts of treasures:

iron and gold ingots, helmets, chest plates, and boots.

The blacksmith carefully slid a pickaxe out of the chest. But then Will saw something else: a shiny iron sword.

*That would be way better than my wooden sword,* he thought, fingering the emeralds in his pocket.

He knew exactly what Seth would tell him to do. He'd say to get the pickaxe, because it was better for building.

But Will couldn't take his eyes off that shiny sword.

By the time he stepped back outside, he'd made the trade. And with the iron sword strapped to his side, he felt ready for anything. Zombies and creepers? No problem. Skeletons and Endermen? *Let me at 'em,* thought Will with a grin.

He was so lost in his thoughts that he ran right into a farmer crossing his path. A few apples fell out of the farmer's cart.

"Oh, sorry!" Will said quickly.

The farmer looked angry, until he got a good look at Will's face. "Oh! You're the builder's brother!"

Will fought the urge to lie. He nodded, smiled, and stepped around the farmer.

*Don't trust strangers,* Seth had told him. But right now, Will couldn't wait to meet a few strangers. He couldn't wait to get out of Little Oak, to a place where no one knew him *or* his famous brother.

He hoisted his pack on his back and walked east toward the still-rising sun.

# CHAPTER 3

Will crested the top of his third hill before looking back. He'd been walking for hours, and the sun was now behind him. He shaded his eyes and glanced back.

He could barely make it out—the black lookout tower of his brother's house. It was a dark, tiny sliver on a distant hill, but he could still see it. Will sighed. He had traveled far today, but not far enough.

"I'll just stop for a snack," he told himself as he sat down on a hollow log. He reached deep into his bag and pulled out what was left of his fish, fruit, and bread.

As he stared at the food in front of him, Will thought of his brother again. Seth would save the food for when he was really hungry. In fact, Seth would probably be building a shelter right now.

"Well I'm not Seth!" Will said out loud. "It's too early to build a shelter. And I'll eat all the food I want—I can always fish for more." He picked up the apple and took a big bite, just to spite his brother. Then he gathered his stuff and started walking again, toward the thick cluster of trees below.

As he pushed through a row of bushes, he found himself at the edge of a lake. Drops of water pinged off its surface. *Rain?* Will looked up and felt a drop on his nose. *Perfect!* This lake looked good for fishing, and fish were easier to catch in the rain.

As he set up his fishing pole, something scuttled in the bushes nearby. Will froze. He held his breath as a furry black leg stepped out from the leaves, and then another, and another.

"Yeesh!" Will leaped backward.

It was a black spider—a very large one. *But it won't attack me,* Will reminded himself, trying to calm his racing heart. *Spiders only attack at night.* This one barely looked at Will before it scurried back into the trees.

Will made sure the spider was gone. Then he caught his breath and found the perfect fishing rock. He tossed his lure into the water, watching the water ripple around it. Sitting there, with gentle rain falling, he yawned and closed his eyes.

That's when he heard it—the hissing coming from the bush beside him. Only it wasn't a bush at all.

"Creeper!" Will shouted as he yanked his pole back out of the water. He grabbed his sack and sprinted away just as the creeper blew up. Will fell forward, planting his face in the mud.

"Dirty creeper. You ruined a perfectly good fishing day!" Will hollered as he sat up, wiping his face. He scanned the bushes for more of the green monsters, but saw nothing.

Will took a deep breath and looked upward. The rain fell harder now, and it didn't look like it would quit anytime soon. "Maybe it *is* time

# CHAPTER 4

Mud flew this way and that as Will dug madly into the earth. He knew that thunderstorms were bad news. Not only would monsters spawn, but they could be super charged by lightning. He had to finish his shelter *right now*.

He heard the moans of the zombies before he saw them. Two—no, three—staggered across the ground, arms outstretched. Will pulled out his bow and launched arrows, one after another. The first zombie dropped with a grunt.

Will's heart pounded as he turned back toward his shelter. *Zombies are slow,* he told himself. *I can make it—I can finish this in time.* He dug out a few more blocks of dirt. Then he grabbed his bow and arrow and whirled around again.

*Yikes!* The two zombies were just a few feet away. Will dropped his bow and grabbed his sword instead. He stepped forward, swinging the sword. With a few strong strokes, he took down the first monster. The iron sword was amazing!

With a surge of confidence, Will attacked the second zombie. The monster growled and groaned before falling backward, dropping chunks of rotten flesh.

Will pumped his sword toward the sky. "Yeah!" he shouted. "Take that, you dirty mobs!"

When he turned back toward his shelter, another bolt of lightning struck. As the blue flash of light hit the ground

in front of him, the hair stood up on Will's arms. *Did I get hit?* he wondered with horror.

Then he saw it—the creeper looming before him. Except this was no ordinary creeper. Lit with an eerie blue light, the super-charged creeper started to sizzle.

Will took a split second to grab his bow and his bag of tools, but it was a split second too long. The explosion lifted him off the ground and ripped everything out of his hands. He sailed toward the lake and hit the ground. *Hard.*

For a moment, he lay perfectly still. He heard nothing. He felt nothing. Then his ears flooded with noise: rain, thunder, and the groaning and hissing of mobs all around.

Without his weapons, Will had no choice. He had to run and hide. But where?

*Water. You'll be safe in the water.* He crawled toward the edge of the lake and plunged in just as an arrow whizzed overhead.

The cold water took Will's breath away. He surfaced a few feet from

shore and heard the *thwang* of another
arrow. Skeletons! They surrounded the
lake, their bows raised. Will gulped
down some air and dove back under.

He swam in circles, but there was
nowhere to go!

He held his breath
till his lungs ached.
When he finally
popped back
up, a *crack* of
lightning lit
up the lake.
That's when he
saw it—the outline of a
wooden boat.

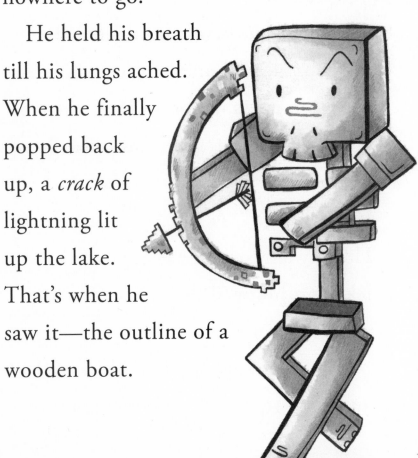

Will dove back under and swam with all his might. Finally, his outstretched hands found the wooden planks of the boat. He used his last bit of strength to pull himself over the edge.

As arrows sailed overhead, Will tumbled into the hull of the boat. He tucked himself into a small, wet ball.

*This,* he thought with a shiver, *is going to be a very long night.*

# CHAPTER 5

*What a terrible dream,* thought Will, stretching. *I can't wait to tell Seth!*

He squinted into the morning light and saw a branch dangling overhead. Where was the dirt roof of his hut? Will sat straight up.

"Oh, man," he said, grabbing the sides of the rocking boat. *It wasn't a dream!* His empty stomach churned with the water around him.

Will's blood boiled with anger. He knew he could avoid the creeper. It was far enough away. But instead, Will grabbed his sword and charged.

Angry words spilled from his lips as he ran. "You good-for-nothing creeper! You ruined my fishing. You ruined my house. You ruined my night. You ruin *everything*!"

But just before he could reach the creeper, someone stepped in front of him. The red-haired girl seemed to come from out of nowhere. She pulled something from her sack and launched it at the creeper.

Will heard the smash of glass. The creeper toppled over, leaving nothing but a trail of gunpowder.

"Got 'im!" said the girl with a triumphant look on her face. She tossed her ponytail over her shoulder and put her hands on her hips. "Hi, I'm Mina."

"I didn't need your help," spat Will. The words came out harsher than he'd intended. "I was going to destroy that creeper myself!"

Mina took a step back. "For your information, I wasn't trying to help you," she said. "I was trying to collect more of *this* for my splash potions." She knelt down and started scraping gunpowder from the ground.

"Splash potions?" Will couldn't help asking.

"Sure," said Mina. "You know—like the splash potion of harming that I just used to take out that creeper. I also brew splash potions of weakness, slowness, poison. . ." She counted them off on her fingers.

Will raised his eyebrows. He'd never met a potion maker before.

As Mina collected the last of the gunpowder, she turned to him and asked, "Do you live around here?"

Will glanced at the burned-out hole in the hill behind him. "Nope." He started to walk back toward the hole to gather his things.

"So where are you from?" asked Mina, falling into step beside him.

"Little Oak," said Will, hoping Mina had never heard of the tiny village.

Her eyes widened. "Hey, that's where that famous builder lives, isn't it?" she said. "Do you know him?"

Will groaned inside. So much for meeting strangers who wouldn't know Seth. He shook his head and changed the subject. "Actually, I've got to get going. I'm on my way to the jungle."

Mina stopped him in his tracks. "No way," she said. "So am I. We can go together!"

*Great.* Will's stomach sunk. He remembered the way Mina had stepped in front of him to kill that creeper. Did she think he needed her protection?

*Like I told Seth, I don't need a babysitter,* Will grumbled to himself. *I can survive on my own.* But would he ever get the chance to prove it?

# CHAPTER 6

Will gazed at the trees stretching toward
the sky. They were getting taller now.
Thicker, too, and covered with lush
green vines. *I made it!* thought Will. A
shiver of excitement ran down his spine.

But as he quickened his step, he
heard Mina right behind him. I *didn't*
*make it.* We *made it,* he corrected
himself with a sigh. Mina had no
trouble keeping up.

"I'm hoping we discover a jungle temple," she said. "Usually you can find pretty cool treasures inside, like gold. I need that to make glistering melon for my healing potions."

*Glistering melon?* Will's stomach twisted with hunger. He thought about asking Mina if she had any of that melon with her right now, but he didn't. She already thought she'd saved him from that creeper. He didn't want her to think she had to feed him too.

"Stop!" Mina suddenly whispered. Will whirled around, expecting to come face to face with a monster. Instead, Mina was pointing at . . .

"A cat?" asked Will. He could barely see the spotted cat prowling in the thicket of trees.

"Not yet," Mina whispered. "He's an ocelot now—a wild cat. But if I feed him a little fish, I might be able to tame him."

"You have fish?" asked Will. His mouth watered at the thought.

But Mina didn't seem to hear him. She pulled a piece of fish from her pack and crouched low, calling softly to the ocelot.

Its green eyes peered at her from behind the trees, but as soon as she took a step forward, the cat ducked into the bushes. There were hanging vines and tall grasses everywhere—so many places for a cat to hide.

Mina tried again and again. She stalked the cat around a small pond. She even tossed her fish toward the ocelot, but every time she got close, it darted away again.

"It's not working," Will said for the third time.

his line again into the water, hoping for better luck.

The bobber ducked underwater instantly. "Already?" said Will, gripping his pole. "Please don't be a pufferfish. Please don't be a pufferfish," he chanted as he reeled in the line.

As the fish broke the surface of the water, he breathed a sigh of relief.

It was a beautiful pink salmon. He could almost taste it now! But as he unhooked the fish, Will had an uneasy feeling—like he was being watched.

He lifted his gaze and saw two green eyes staring back at him through the tall grass beside the water. The cat blinked slowly and took a step forward.

Will swallowed hard. He wasn't the only one who wanted that salmon.

# CHAPTER 7

The ocelot was so close now, Will
could almost see the saliva dripping
off its sharp teeth. He sucked in his
breath. *What do I do?* He didn't have a
clue, but he knew someone who did.

The last thing he wanted was to ask Mina for help. *Actually,* he thought, *the last thing I want is to get eaten by an ocelot.* So he swallowed his pride and whispered, "What do I do?"

"Hold the fish steady," whispered Mina. "Don't move."

Will's hand shook, but he kept it outstretched.

The ocelot crouched low and took a slow step forward, as if he were stalking the salmon. Then he took another step. And another.

When the cat was just feet away, Will couldn't help it—he dropped the fish and snatched his hand back.

"Don't scare it away!" Mina cried.

But she didn't have to worry. The ocelot pounced on the fish and gobbled it up. Then he licked his paw, cleaned his face, and sat down in front of Will as if he were a sweet little kitten.

Mina shook her head. "I can't believe he chose you," she said. "After I tried so hard!"

Will shrugged. "You can have him." He still couldn't take his eyes off the cat, as if it were going to turn wild again any moment now.

Mina groaned. "It doesn't work that way! He's yours now. He'll only follow you."

"What?" Will whirled around to face Mina. "That's dumb—I don't believe that." To prove his point, he packed up his fishing gear and headed toward the trees. But sure enough, when he glanced over his shoulder, the cat was following him. And Mina too. Will felt like he was leading a cat parade.

He stopped short. "What am I supposed to do with a pet cat out here in the jungle?"

Mina narrowed her eyes. "You take care of him, that's what. And he takes care of you too, by keeping the creepers away. Creepers can't stand cats."

Will paused. He'd be glad to never see another creeper, that's for sure. But when he looked down at the cat, he wondered again, *What do I do with him?* He shook his head. "I told you, I don't want him," he said firmly.

Mina's face scrunched up with anger. "I can't believe you tamed an ocelot—something I've *always* wanted to do. And you don't even appreciate him!" Her voice bounced off the trees.

"Well I never asked for a pet cat!" Will shot back. "I never asked for either one of you to come with me. You just slow me down!" The words tumbled out so fast he couldn't stop them.

Mina pulled back, as if he'd shot her with an arrow. "Fine," she said in a trembling voice. "I won't go with you, then." She  took a step in the other direction. "Enjoy the jungle, Will."

But as he pushed through the tangled vines and bushes, he realized something: he wasn't sure anymore which way was forward and which way was backward!

Will spun in a long slow circle, panic rising in his chest. His cat just sat on the ground nearby, watching and waiting.

"What do we do now, Shadow?" Will asked, trying to keep his voice steady.

*Build shelter.* The answer came to him quickly, and he knew that it was the right one. *It's what Seth would do—and it'll keep us safe.*

Will searched for a hillside to burrow into, but there wasn't one.

He saw plenty of wood for building, but no space in between the trees to build. Now what?

He stared at the sky, hoping for inspiration—and he got it. If he couldn't build a house on the ground, he'd have to build one *off* the ground. A house in the trees. A tree house!

Will ran his hand over the thick net of vines wrapped around the nearest tree trunk. Was it thick enough to climb? "Only one way to find out," he said out loud. He grabbed a hold of one vine while stepping onto another. Then he began creeping slowly up the side of the tree.

A few feet up, he realized he'd
forgotten something. He glanced
back at the ground, where the cat was
waiting patiently.

"Well, Shadow," said Will with a
smile, "are you
coming, or
what?"

# CHAPTER 8

By the time darkness fell, Will had
built a crude tree house—a platform
under the canopy of leaves at the
top of the tree. Vines hung down all
around like green, leafy walls.

"Not bad, is it, Shadow?" Will asked.

The cat blinked a slow reply.

"I mean, I know Seth could build a better one." Will closed his eyes and imagined the amazing tree house Seth might have built. It had walls and windows, lots of levels, and a rope bridge leading to a nearby tree.

"But Seth's not here," Will reminded himself. "So I did the best I could." He lit a torch and settled back to wait.

When he felt the pains of hunger, he remembered the salmon he had caught hours ago. "I'm starving," he said, "but you're not, are you, Shadow? You have a belly full of delicious fish. *My* fish."

Shadow meowed an apology and rubbed his head against Will's hand.

Then they both heard it—the first distant moan. As the grumbles and groans grew louder, the cat leapt up and began pacing.

"It's okay," said Will. "Zombies can't climb trees. We don't have to worry about them."

He didn't tell Shadow what they *did* have to worry about. It wasn't the skeletons, because they couldn't see through the vine walls. *It's the spiders,* he thought with a shudder. They could climb trees. He swallowed a lump of fear and snuck a quick peek over the edge of the platform.

The zombies were down there in full force now. They grunted and bobbled around, running into the base of the tree. Will took a deep breath

and reached for his bow and arrow.
Then he leaned back over the edge.

*Thwap! Thwap! Thwap!* He took
out the zombies easily. They were like
sitting ducks! Soon, rotten flesh littered
the ground. But one of the zombies
had dropped something else: a carrot.

Will's mouth watered. He was so hungry! Could he climb down and get the carrot before more mobs showed up?

*Thwack!* An arrow struck the platform just beside Will's hand. He yanked his arm back inside the vines and listened to the rattling of skeleton bones below. Then he heard something else: a low growl from *inside* the tree house.

Will turned his head slowly in the darkness and saw two glowing eyes. Was it an Enderman? A bolt of fear ran through Will's chest. He quickly looked away.

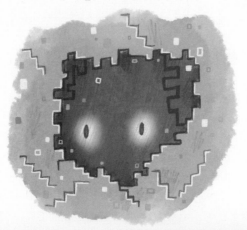

*Never look an Enderman in the eye,* he reminded himself. But was it too late? He held his breath.

Then those eyes appeared again. Two *green* eyes—not purple. It was the *cat* who was growling at the mobs below.

Will blew out a sigh of relief. "It's okay," he whispered to Shadow. "You're safe in here with me." He only wished it were true.

Arrows pinged off the wooden platform, and then came the sound Will had been dreading—the scuttle of spider legs.

He jumped to his feet. How many were there? He swallowed his panic and dared to look over the edge.

# CHAPTER 9

Will whipped his bow at the spider—it was all he could do! Then he fumbled around in the dark for his sword.

Just as his hand gripped the handle, he heard a snapping sound overhead. The vines were breaking. The spider was crawling into the shelter.

Will jumped out of the spider's path and tugged his sword hard from its sheath—too hard. The sword flew from his hand and skipped across the tree house floor. He watched with sickening horror as the sword slid through a gap in the vines and disappeared into the darkness.

As the spider hissed and crawled toward him, Will's arms flailed, searching for weapons that he no longer had.

*Run!* he told himself. But where?

He teetered on the edge of the platform, wondering if he could survive the fall.

Then the monster stopped and scurried sideways—away from Will.

Cool relief washed over him, until he realized what had distracted the spider.

*Shadow.*

The cat growled from a far corner of the tree house. Would he fight the spider? Will didn't wait to find out.

He felt a surge of anger and rushed toward the creature, pounding its furry body with his fists.

The spider hissed, spun around, and flung Will to the ground.

Then it was standing over him, surrounding him with its legs, glowering down at him with fiery red eyes.

*This is it,* thought Will, closing his eyes. *This is how I die.*

Then he heard the whiz of an arrow and the grunt of the monster being struck, square in the heart.

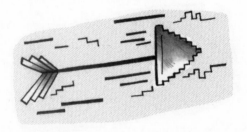

But it wasn't Will's arrow. It wasn't his bow.

"Who's there?" he shouted, sliding his body backward just as the dying spider toppled to the floor.

A familiar voice rang out in the darkness. "It's me. It's Mina." A lit torch suddenly bobbed into view. *But no one was holding it.*

Will whirled around. "Where are you?" he hollered. "I can't see you!"

"I drank a potion of invisibility," Mina explained. "Now stop moving around or you'll fall off the edge. Are you okay? Are you hurt?"

Will squeezed his fingers against his forehead, trying to figure out what had just happened. "I'm okay—I think. But how long have you been here?" he asked.

As Mina slowly reappeared, she shrugged. "Not long. I mean, I was following you. But I didn't come into the tree house until just a few minutes ago. It was safer in here than out there, with all the mobs."

Something clicked in Will's mind. "So the cat was looking at *you*!" he said. "That's why he was acting so weird. . . ." His voice trailed off to a whisper as he sat back down. Suddenly, he was feeling pretty weird himself.

"What's wrong?" Mina asked. "Are you mad that I followed you? Did you *not* want my help killing that spider?"

Will felt a wave of tiredness. He was too sleepy to respond.

"I wasn't only trying to help you," Mina went on. "I was also trying to

collect more
of these."
She bent
down to pick
up two spider
eyes, all that
was left of the
dead spider now. "I

use them in almost all of my potions."

Will wanted to say something to
Mina, something really important.
But he couldn't remember what it
was. As the room began to spin, he
fell backward. He heard a *thunk* and
felt a stab of pain as his head hit the
wooden floor.

finally remembered that important thing he had to tell his friend. "Mina," he said softly. "I *did* need your help with the spider. It's a good thing you showed up when you did. I made a real mess of things here in the jungle."

Mina cocked her head. "What do you mean?"

Will sighed. "My brother was right—I didn't have a plan. I wanted to have an adventure, but I almost got killed. And I put you and the cat in danger, too."

"No, you didn't mess up!" said Mina. "You fought off a ton of mobs before that spider jockey came along. You built this cool tree house, which gave me a place to hide tonight. And best of all, you kept your cat safe." She reached out and scratched the cat under the chin.

Will smiled. "His name is Shadow. And I think he kept me safe, too. I haven't seen a single creeper since that cat came along."

"I told you!" said Mina, punching Will playfully in the arm.

He laughed. "You were right," he said. "Having a pet cat is pretty cool."

"And *you* were right about something," said Mina. "It's good to have adventures. But maybe it's good to plan ahead a little, too."

Will made a face. "You mean like plan to bring enough food so that you don't have to eat spider eyes?" He grimaced.

Mina giggled. "Yeah, like that." As a shaft of light spilled across the tree house floor, she pulled aside the vines to peek outside. "The sun is up. Do you want to make a plan for today? Maybe we can find that jungle temple."

Will didn't have to think about it. He shook his head. "I want to see the temple someday, but there's somewhere else I need to go first."

"Where?" asked Mina.

As Will said the word, he felt something warm burst inside his chest. "Home."

# CHAPTER 10

"Which way?" asked Will. He had followed the sun to get to the jungle, but he couldn't follow the sun to get home. He couldn't even *see* the sun through the leaves of the jungle trees. They were too thick and tall!

"Follow the arrows," said Mina. She pointed to a nearby tree trunk, which had a small arrow scratched into its side.

"Who did that?" asked Will.

"I did!" said Mina. "On the way here. I always mark my trails when I'm exploring."

Will grinned. *Have adventures, but have a plan too,* Mina had said. And she sure knew how to plan ahead.

They followed the arrows all the way to the edge of the jungle. This time, Mina led the cat parade, and Will and Shadow brought up the rear.

Mina nodded. "I think so. But wait! I have an idea." She dug through her bag and pulled out a glass bottle, which held a splash of golden yellow liquid. "A potion of water breathing," she explained. She took a quick sip and handed it to Will.

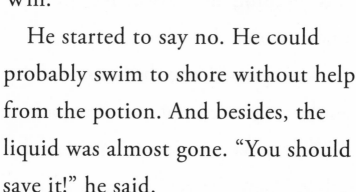

He started to say no. He could probably swim to shore without help from the potion. And besides, the liquid was almost gone. "You should save it!" he said.

"You gave me a pufferfish so that I could make more, remember?" said Mina. "We make a great team."

Will couldn't argue with that. As the water rose in the boat, he stared into Shadow's emerald eyes. "You're part of the team, too," he reminded the cat. "You have to follow us to shore, okay? You *have* to."

Then he chugged down the fishy-tasting potion and jumped overboard.

As Will dove down deep, he heard two more splashes from up above. There was Mina, swimming down to meet him. And along the surface of the water, four cat paws paddled toward shore.

Will smiled with relief. Then he opened his mouth to take his first breath. It flowed into his lungs, cool as the morning air. *Am I dreaming?* he wondered as he blew the breath back out. An orange clownfish flitted past, dodging the bubbles.

For just a moment, Will remembered that other night—when lightning had lit up the sky and he had hid in this water, scared and lonely. He did an underwater somersault to shake off the memory.

*I'll have more adventures,* he told himself. *But maybe next time, I won't go it alone.*

Then he fluttered his feet and followed Mina toward shore.